COMIN' DOWN TO STORYTIME

Rob Reid

Pictures by

Nadine Bernard Westcott

UpstartBooks

Janesville, Wisconsin
www.upstartbooks.com

Published by UpstartBooks
401 S. Wright Road
P.O. Box 5207
Janesville, Wisconsin 53547-5207
1-800-448-4887

Text © 2009 by Rob Reid
Illustrations © 2009 by Nadine Bernard Westcott

*To all of the children who not only sat in
my story programs over the years, but also sang,
jumped, hollered, danced, and laughed along with me.*
—R. R.

For Will and Kendall.
— N. B. W.

We'll be comin' down to storytime when we come. Yee ha!
Yes, we'll be comin' down to storytime when we come. Yee ha!

We'll be comin' down to storytime,
We'll be comin' down to storytime,
We'll be comin' down to storytime when we come. Yee ha!

We will hear a funny story when we come. Ha! Ha!
Yes, we'll hear a funny story when we come. Ha! Ha!
We will hear a funny story,
We will hear a funny story,

We will hear a funny story when we come. Ha! Ha!

We will say a nursery rhyme when we come. Mother Goose!
Yes, we'll say a nursery rhyme when we come. Mother Goose!

We will say a nursery rhyme,
We will say a nursery rhyme,
We will say a nursery rhyme when we come. Mother Goose!

We will make a fingerplay when we come. Itsy Bitsy!
Yes, we'll make a fingerplay when we come. Itsy Bitsy!

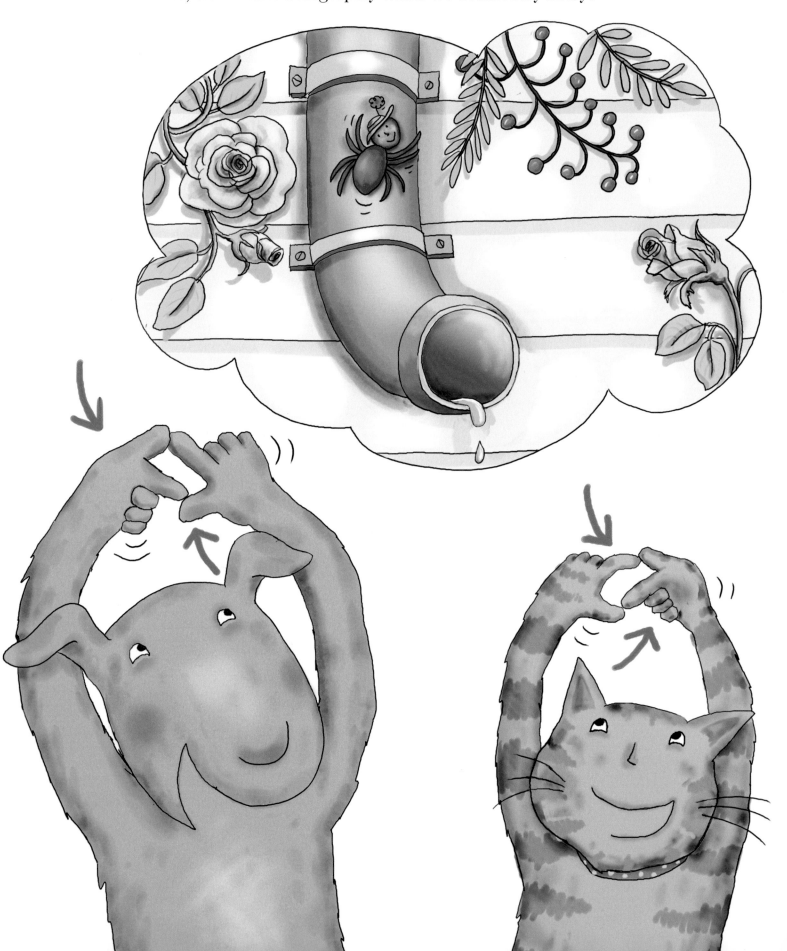

We will make a fingerplay,

We will make a fingerplay,

We will make a fingerplay when we come. Itsy Bitsy!

We will sing a little song when we come. La! La!

Yes, we'll sing a little song when we come. La! La!

We will sing a little song,

We will sing a little song,

We will sing a little song when we come. La! La!

We will "Quack" and we will "Moo" when we come. Quack! Moo!
Yes, we will "Quack" and we will "Moo" when we come. Quack! Moo!

We will "Quack" and we will "Moo,"
We will "Quack" and we will "Moo,"
We will "Quack" and we will "Moo" when we come. Quack! Moo!

We will all join hands and move when we come. Skip to my Lou!

Yes, we'll all join hands and move when we come. Skip to my Lou!
We will all join hands and move,
We will all join hands and move,
We will all join hands and move when we come. Skip to my Lou!

We will make a pretty picture when we come. Draw! Draw!
Yes, we'll make a pretty picture when we come. Draw! Draw!
We will make a pretty picture,
We will make a pretty picture,
We will make a pretty picture when we come. Draw! Draw!

We might even get a treat when we come. Yum! Yum!
Yes, we might even get a treat when we come. Yum! Yum!

We might even get a treat,
We might even get a treat,
We might even get a treat when we come. Yum! Yum!

We will check out lots of books when we leave. Bye now!
Yes, we'll check out lots of books when we leave. Bye now!
We will check out lots of books,
We will check out lots of books,

We will check out lots of books when we leave.

Bye now!